HISTORY SPEAKS
PICTURE BOOKS PLUS READER'S THEATER

Ellen Craft's
ESCAPE FROM SLAVERY

BY **CATHY MOORE**
ILLUSTRATED BY **MARK BRAUGHT**

M MILLBROOK PRESS / MINNEAPOLIS

In memory of Ellen and William Craft ——CM

To everyone who has strived, and continues to strive, to make "I have a dream" a reality ——MB

Millbrook Press
A division of Lerner Publishing Group, Inc.
241 First Avenue North
Minneapolis, MN 55401 U.S.A.

Website address: www.lernerbooks.com

The map in this book is used with the permission of: © Laura Westlund/ Independent Picture Service, p. 33.

Library of Congress Cataloging-in-Publication Data
Moore, Cathy, 1961–
    Ellen Craft's escape from slavery / by Cathy Moore ; illustrated by Mark Braught.
       p.   cm. — (History speaks : picture books plus reader's theater)
    Includes bibliographical references.
    ISBN 978–0–7613–5875–6 (lib. bdg. : alk. paper)
    1. Craft, Ellen—Juvenile literature. 2. Craft, William—Juvenile literature.
3. Fugitive slaves—United States—Biography—Juvenile literature.
4. Fugitive slaves—England—Biography—Juvenile literature. 5. Slaves—
Georgia—Biography—Juvenile literature. 6. African Americans—
Biography—Juvenile literature. 7. Readers' theater—Juvenile literature. I.
Title.
E450.C79M67 2011
920.009296073—dc22   2010001721

Manufactured in the United States of America
1 – CG – 7/15/10

CONTENTS

MACON, GEORGIA

➤ *December 1848* ➤

Christmas was coming soon. The Collins family was looking forward to parties and presents. For Ellen Craft, Christmas just meant more work.

She was a slave in the home of Master and Missus Collins. Missus Collins had kept Ellen busy all day. Ellen was grateful when night came. At last, she could go home.

Ellen was bone tired. She walked along the shadowy path to her tiny home. Ellen shared a cabin with her husband, William. He was a slave too. Ellen hated being a slave. Slaves had no freedom. They could be bought and sold like animals.

Even children could be sold and sent away from their parents. Ellen had been taken away from her mother when she was a little girl. When she married William, Ellen made a promise.

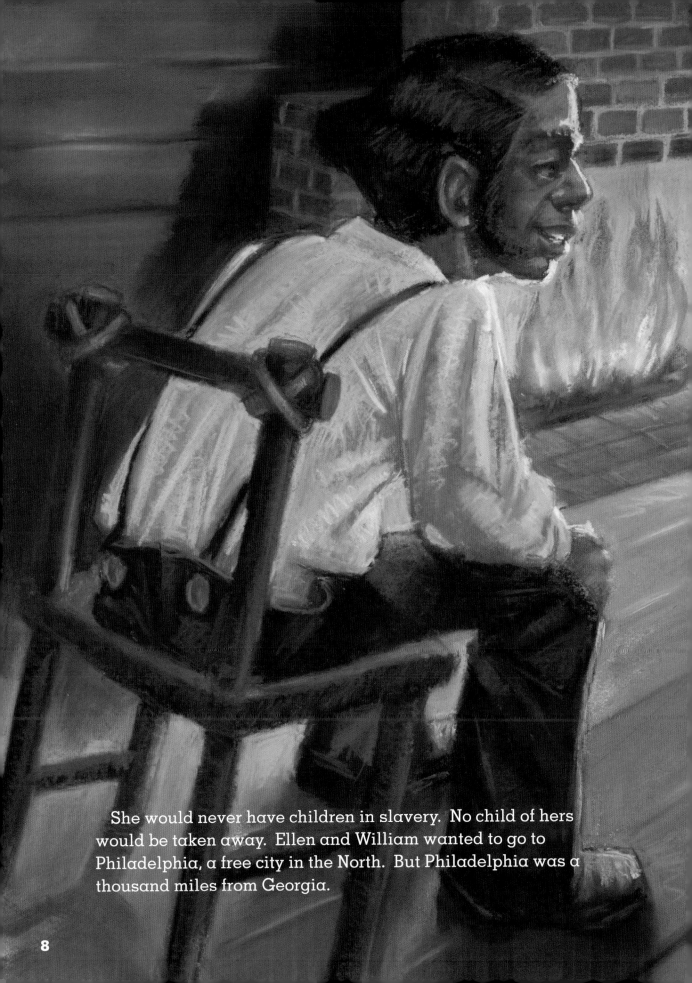

She would never have children in slavery. No child of hers would be taken away. Ellen and William wanted to go to Philadelphia, a free city in the North. But Philadelphia was a thousand miles from Georgia.

Ellen and William had talked about running away many times. Now they sat by the fire and talked once more. Most runaways were caught before they reached freedom.

They could be sold off or beaten terribly. Sometimes slaves who fought back were killed. Ellen and William decided they would rather die than be slaves. They went over ideas for escape. All their old ideas seemed impossible.

Suddenly William grabbed Ellen's hand. Her skin was light against his dark hand. She could pretend to be white, William said. And William could travel as her slave. But quickly, Ellen saw a problem. A white woman would never travel alone with a male slave. Ellen would have to pretend to be a white man. They would have to travel many miles and fool many people. It was their only chance for freedom. They had to try.

The next day, Ellen and William asked for Christmas
passes. Some masters gave these out so slaves could visit
relatives in other places. Ellen and William got passes to
leave on December 21. But they had to be back on the day after
Christmas. They had five days to get to Philadelphia. After
that, slave catchers would start hunting for them.

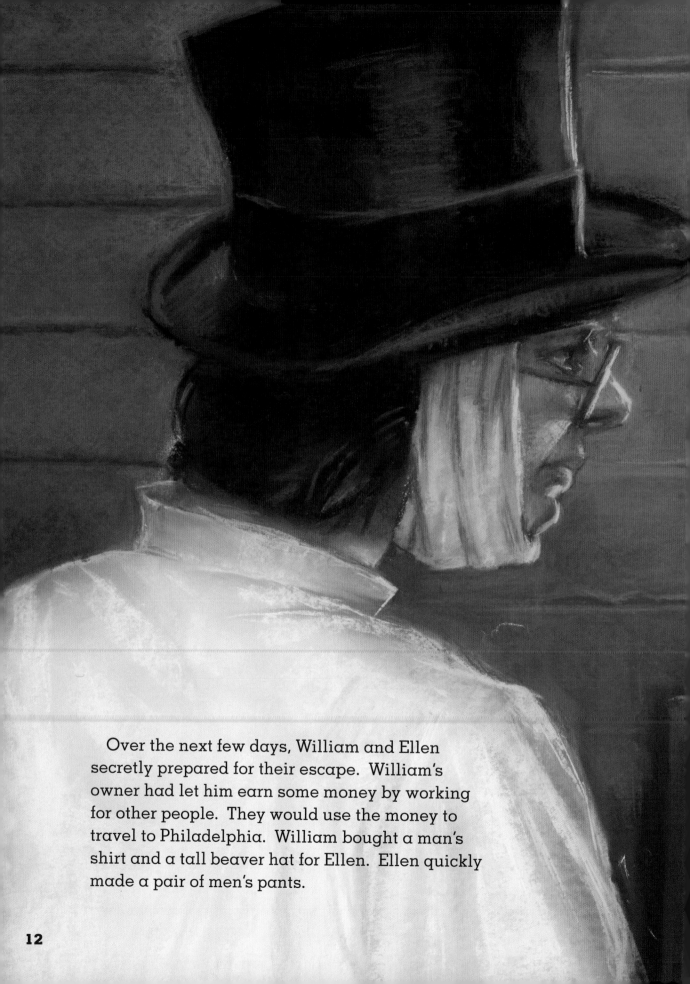

Over the next few days, William and Ellen secretly prepared for their escape. William's owner had let him earn some money by working for other people. They would use the money to travel to Philadelphia. William bought a man's shirt and a tall beaver hat for Ellen. Ellen quickly made a pair of men's pants.

On their last night in the cabin, William snipped off
Ellen's hair. Then Ellen put on the men's clothes and the
tall hat.

Ellen looked in the mirror. She still looked like a woman.
She wrapped some bandages around her head. They hid
her smooth face. She added dark glasses. They hid her
scared eyes.

Ellen had one more thing to hide. A white gentleman would
be able to write. But Ellen didn't know how to write. So Ellen
put her arm in a sling. If she had to sign something, she would
ask someone to do it for her.

The bandages and sling made Ellen look sick. She would say she was traveling to see a good doctor. She would call herself Mr. Johnson. Ellen and William spent the whole night going over their plan. Finally, dawn came.

Ellen took a deep breath. She lifted her chin and pushed her hat into place. Then she stepped outside. Ellen and William walked separately to the train station nearby. They met at the ticket window. Ellen asked for two tickets. One for herself and one for her slave. The agent asked no questions.

Ellen took the tickets and held them tight. She couldn't ride with William. He had to ride in the railroad car for slaves. Ellen would travel in a car for white passengers. She was on her own now.

White men filled Ellen's car. They were smoking and chatting.
Then a white man sat down next to her.

"It is a very fine morning, sir," he said.

Ellen's heart pounded. She knew this man. He was
Mr. Cray. Mr. Cray had known Ellen since she was little.

Ellen turned her face to the window. At first, she pretended she was deaf. But Mr. Cray kept asking her questions. Ellen made her voice low and calm. She answered Mr. Cray. He never guessed she was a runaway slave.

In Savannah, Georgia, Ellen and William boarded
a boat bound for South Carolina. It was a cold night.
There was no place for black people to sleep on the boat.
William had to sleep on some cotton bundles on deck.

Ellen stayed in a clean, warm bed. All night, she lay awake.
She had been Mr. Johnson for one day. She had four days to go.
When morning came, Ellen wanted to hide in bed. But she had
to go to breakfast and face the white men there.

William helped Ellen into the dining room. He called her "master" and "sir." Ellen had to act like a master. But she thanked William for everything he did. "You're going to spoil your slave," one man warned Ellen.

"You have to treat slaves like dogs. You have to yell. You have
to scare them. Otherwise, they get proud and run away."

The other men at breakfast agreed. Ellen wanted to shout,
Slaves are not dogs! But she just nodded. She talked about her
health instead.

In Charleston, William and Ellen ate dinner in a hotel.
William had to eat in the kitchen. Ellen was served by two
slaves in the fancy dining room. She had to act like Mr. Johnson.
But she thanked them kindly and handed them extra money.
Soon it was time to go to the ticket office in town.

Ellen asked for tickets to Philadelphia. The ticket agent wanted to be certain William belonged to Mr. Johnson. He knew that some white people helped runaway slaves travel to freedom. The agent gave Mr. Johnson a form to sign.

Ellen pointed at the sling. She said she couldn't use her arm. Would the ticket agent sign the form instead? The agent refused. He didn't do favors for strangers, he said. Ellen didn't know what to do.

Finally, a man from the boat trip said William was Mr.
Johnson's slave. Someone signed the form. Ellen and William
were one step closer to freedom.

For two more days, William and Ellen traveled by boat
and train. Ellen worried about getting to Philadelphia by
Christmas Day.

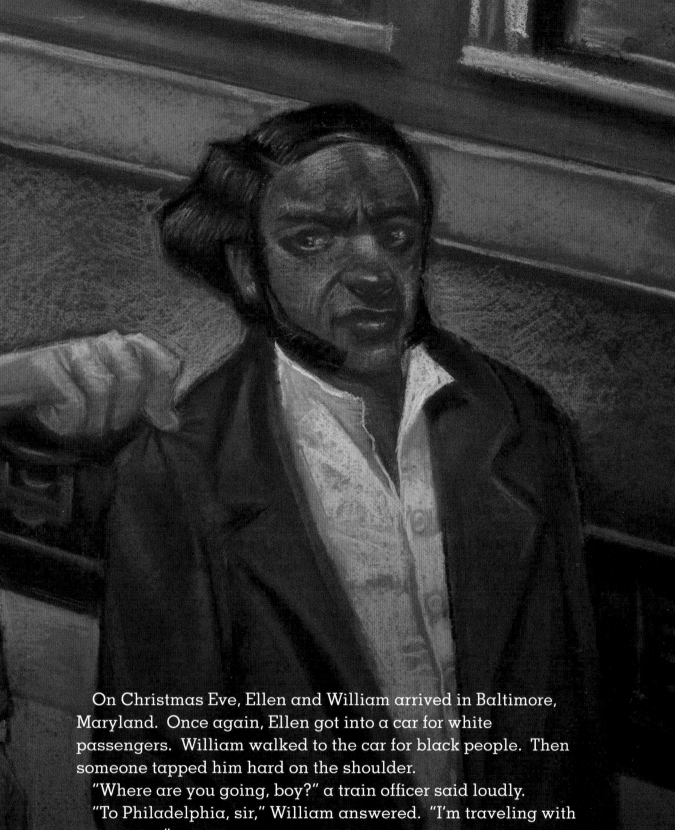

On Christmas Eve, Ellen and William arrived in Baltimore, Maryland. Once again, Ellen got into a car for white passengers. William walked to the car for black people. Then someone tapped him hard on the shoulder.

"Where are you going, boy?" a train officer said loudly.

"To Philadelphia, sir," William answered. "I'm traveling with my master."

"Well, you'd better get him into the office," the man said. "You have to get approval first."

William and Ellen walked to the office. The railroad officer
looked serious. He wasn't going to let any slaves escape to the
North from his station.

He wanted proof that William really belonged to Mr. Johnson.
Ellen said she didn't have any proof. The officer asked if Mr.
Johnson knew anyone in Baltimore who could help.

"No," Ellen said.

A crowd had gathered outside the office.

Ellen tried hard not to panic. What would a white man do? she thought. A white man would not be afraid. A white man would be angry. He would demand better treatment. So Ellen did something a slave could never do. She stood up for her rights.

"I bought tickets all the way to Philadelphia," she said angrily. "You have no right to keep me here!"

The people in the crowd agreed.

Just then, the bell clanged. It was time for the train to leave. "I give up," the train officer said finally. "I suppose it's all right." William and Ellen hurried onto the train. In a few hours, it would be Christmas Day.

Early on Christmas morning, Ellen saw lights in the distance. It was Philadelphia! As soon as the train stopped, William and Ellen climbed off. Ellen looked around at the other passengers. People were laughing and hugging their families.

We can be a family now, Ellen thought. We're finally safe. We'll never be slaves again. Ellen took William's arm. And they walked together toward the free streets of Philadelphia.

Author's Note

After a rest in Philadelphia, Ellen and William moved to Boston, Massachusetts. William worked as a carpenter, and Ellen worked as a seamstress. They also joined the movement known as abolitionism. Abolitionists worked to bring an end to slavery.

William and Ellen gave speeches about their escape and about the cruelties of slavery. They wanted to convince people that slavery should end. Soon they were famous in the North— and in the South. The Crafts' owners found out where they were and sent slave hunters to capture William and Ellen.

The Crafts fled to Britain, where slavery was illegal. Truly safe, they could at last start their family. The Crafts had the first of five children in 1852. They also continued to give speeches. William even wrote a book about their escape. *Running a Thousand Miles for Freedom: The Escape of William and Ellen Craft from Slavery* was published in 1860.

After the Civil War (1861–1865), Ellen wanted to help the newly freed slaves. By 1870, the Crafts were back in Georgia. This time, however, they owned a plantation—and a school for black children. But money trouble and threats by whites made their work very hard. After about nineteen years, the Crafts moved to Charleston, South Carolina, where they lived their final days in peace.

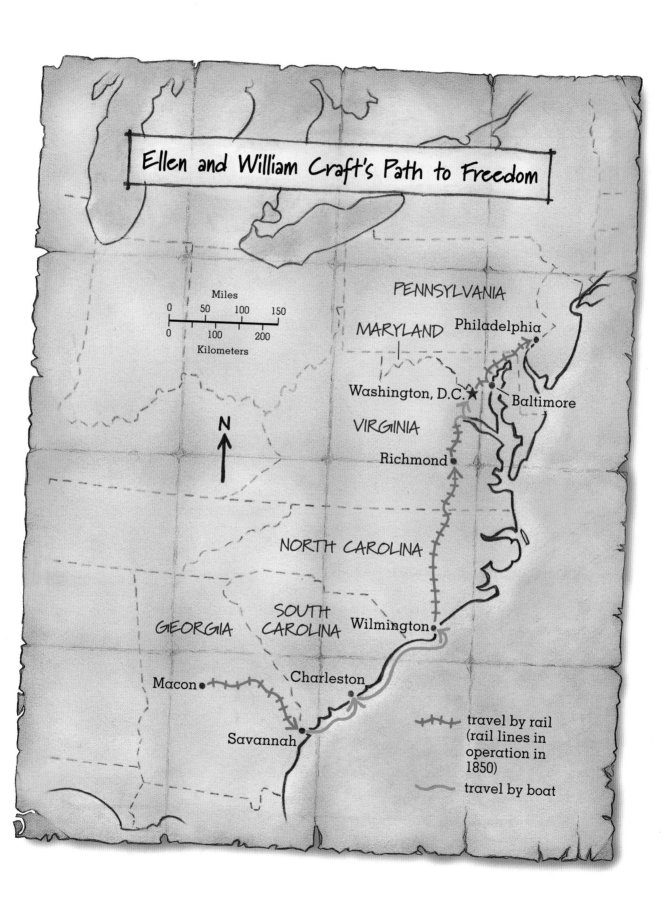

Ellen and William Craft's Path to Freedom

Miles
0   50   100   150
0   100   200
Kilometers

N

PENNSYLVANIA

MARYLAND   Philadelphia

Washington, D.C. ★   Baltimore

VIRGINIA

Richmond

NORTH CAROLINA

GEORGIA   SOUTH
CAROLINA   Wilmington

Macon •   Charleston

Savannah

travel by rail
(rail lines in
operation in
1850)

travel by boat

Performing Reader's Theater

Dear Student,

Reader's Theater is a dramatic reading. It is a little like a play, but you don't need to memorize your lines. Here are some tips that will help you do your best in a Reader's Theater performance.

BEFORE THE PERFORMANCE

- **Choose your part:** Your teacher may assign parts, or you may be allowed to choose your own part. The character you play does not need to be the same age as you. A boy can play the part of a girl, and a girl can play the part of a boy. That's why it's called acting!

- **Find your lines:** Your character's name is always the same color. The name at the bottom of each page tells you which character has the first line on the next page. If you are allowed to write on your script, highlight your lines. If you cannot write on the script, you may want to use sticky flags to mark your lines.

- **Check pronunciations of words:** If your character's lines include any words you aren't sure how to pronounce, check the pronunciation guide on page 45. If a word isn't there or you still aren't sure how to say it, check a dictionary or ask a teacher, librarian, or other adult.

- **Use your emotions:** Think about how your character feels in the story. If you imagine how your character feels, the audience will hear the emotion in your voice.

- **Use your imagination:** Think about how your character's voice might sound. For example, an old man's voice will sound different from a baby's voice. If you do change your voice, make sure the audience can still understand the words you are saying.

- **Practice your lines:** Even though you do not need to memorize your lines, you should still be comfortable reading them. Read your lines aloud often so they flow smoothly.

DURING THE PERFORMANCE

- **Keep your script away from your face but high enough to read:** If you cover your face with your script, you block your voice from the audience. If you have your script too low, you need to tip your head down farther to read it and the audience won't be able to hear you.

- **Use eye contact:** Good Reader's Theater performers look at the audience as much as they look at their scripts. If you look down, the sound of your voice goes down to the script and not out to the audience.

- **Speak clearly:** Make sure you are loud enough. Say all your words carefully. Be sure not to read too quickly. Remember, if you feel nervous, you may start to speak faster than usual.

- **Use facial expressions and gestures:** Your facial expressions and gestures (hand movements) help the audience know how your character is feeling. If your character is happy, smile. If your character is angry, cross your arms and be sure not to smile.

- **Have fun:** It's okay if you feel nervous. If you make a mistake, just try to relax and keep going. Reader's Theater is meant to be fun for the actors and the audience!

Cast of Characters

NARRATOR 1

NARRATOR 2

ELLEN CRAFT:
a female African American slave

WILLIAM CRAFT:
a male African American slave

READER 1:
Master Collins, man on boat

READER 2:
Missus Collins, Mr. Cray

RAILROAD OFFICER

TICKET AGENT

ALL:
Everyone except sound

SOUND:
This part has no lines. The person in this role
is in charge of the sound effects.
Find the sound effects for this script
at www.historyspeaksbooks.com.

The Script

SOUND: [jingle bells]

NARRATOR 1: It was almost Christmas in Macon, Georgia. The year was 1848. The Collins family was looking forward to parties and presents. But for Ellen Craft, Christmas just meant more work. Ellen was a slave in the home of Master and Missus Collins.

NARRATOR 2: Missus Collins had kept Ellen busy all day. Ellen was grateful when night came. She was bone tired, and at last, she could go home. She walked along the shadowy path to her tiny home. Ellen shared a cabin with her husband, William. He was a slave too.

ELLEN: I hate being a slave. We can be bought and sold like animals. I want freedom!

NARRATOR 1: Even children could be sold as slaves and sent away from their parents. Ellen had been taken away from her mother when she was a little girl. When she married William, Ellen made a promise.

ELLEN: I will never have children in slavery. No child of mine will ever be taken away.

NARRATOR 1: Ellen and William had talked about running away many times. Now they sat by the fire and talked once more.

WILLIAM: We'll escape to a free city in the North, like Philadelphia!

Next Page — **ELLEN**

ELLEN: But Philadelphia is almost one thousand miles from Georgia. If we're caught, we could be sold or beaten. And if we fight back, we could be killed!

WILLIAM: I would rather die than stay a slave.

ELLEN: Me too.

NARRATOR 2: They went over ideas for escape. All their old ideas seemed impossible. Suddenly William grabbed Ellen's hand.

WILLIAM: Your skin is light against my dark hand. You could pretend to be white. And I could travel as your slave.

ELLEN: But a white woman would never travel alone with a male slave. I'll have to pretend to be a white *man*.

WILLIAM: We'll have to travel a long way and fool a lot of people. But it's our only chance for freedom.

ELLEN: We have to try.

NARRATOR 1: The next day, Ellen went to speak with Master and Missus Collins. Some masters gave out Christmas passes so slaves could visit relatives in other places.

ELLEN: Excuse me, Master Collins. I was wondering if I could have a Christmas pass to visit relatives this year.

READER 1 (as Master Collins): I suppose that would be all right. You can leave December 21. Would that be okay with you, Missus Collins?

Next Page — **READER 2**

READER 2 (as Missus Collins): If you say so. But she needs to be back the day after Christmas.

NARRATOR 2: Ellen and William had five days to get to Philadelphia. After that, slave catchers would start hunting for them.

NARRATOR 1: Over the next few days, William and Ellen secretly prepared for their escape. William's owner had let him earn some money by working for other people. They would use the money to travel to Philadelphia. William bought a man's shirt and a tall beaver hat for Ellen. Ellen quickly made a pair of men's pants.

NARRATOR 2: On their last night in the cabin, William snipped off Ellen's hair.

SOUND: [scissors snipping]

NARRATOR 2: Then Ellen put on the men's clothes and the tall hat. She looked in the mirror.

ELLEN: I still look like a woman. Maybe if I wrap bandages around my head, they will hide my face.

WILLIAM: Wear these dark glasses. They'll hide your eyes.

ELLEN: A white gentleman would be able to write. But I don't know how.

WILLIAM: We'll put your arm in a sling. If you have to sign something, you can ask someone to do it for you.

Next Page — **ELLEN**

ELLEN: The bandages and the sling make me look sick. I'll say I am traveling to see a good doctor. I will call myself Mr. Johnson.

NARRATOR 1: Ellen and William spent the whole night going over their plan. Finally, dawn came. Ellen took a deep breath. She lifted her chin, pushed her hat into place, and stepped outside. Ellen and William walked separately to the train station nearby. They met at the ticket window.

ELLEN: Two tickets, please. One for myself and one for my slave.

NARRATOR 2: The agent asked no questions. Ellen took the tickets and held them tight. She couldn't ride with William. He had to ride in the railroad car for slaves. Ellen would travel in a car for white passengers. She was on her own now.

SOUND: [train whistle]

NARRATOR 1: White men filled Ellen's car. They were smoking and chatting. Then a white man sat down next to her.

READER 2 (as Mr. Cray): It's a very fine morning, sir.

NARRATOR 2: Ellen's heart pounded. She knew this man. He was Mr. Cray. Mr. Cray had known Ellen since she was little. Ellen turned her face to the window. At first, she pretended she was deaf. But Mr. Cray kept asking her questions. Ellen made her voice low and calm.

ELLEN: Yes, it is a very fine morning, indeed.

Next Page — **NARRATOR 1**

NARRATOR 1: Mr. Cray never guessed she was a runaway slave.

SOUND: [boat horn]

NARRATOR 2: In Savannah, Georgia, Ellen and William boarded a boat bound for South Carolina. It was a cold night. There was no place for black people to sleep on the boat. William had to sleep on some cotton bundles on deck.

NARRATOR 1: Ellen stayed in a clean, warm bed. All night, she lay awake. She had been Mr. Johnson for one day, and she had four days remaining. When morning came, Ellen wanted to hide in bed. But she had to go to breakfast and face the white men there.

WILLIAM: Here's your breakfast, Master.

ELLEN: Thank you, William.

WILLIAM: Would you like some juice, sir?

ELLEN: Yes, William. Thank you.

NARRATOR 1: One of the boat's passengers warned Ellen that she was being too kind to William.

READER 1 (as man on boat): You're going to spoil your slave. You have to treat slaves like dogs. You have to yell. You have to scare them. Otherwise, they get proud and run away.

NARRATOR 2: The other men at breakfast agreed. Ellen wanted to shout, Slaves are not dogs! But she just nodded. She talked about her health instead.

Next Page — **NARRATOR 1**

NARRATOR 1: In Charleston, William and Ellen ate dinner in a hotel. William had to eat in the kitchen while two slaves served Ellen in the fancy dining room. She had to act like Mr. Johnson. But she thanked them kindly and handed them extra money. Soon it was time to go to the ticket office in town.

ELLEN: Two tickets to Philadelphia, please.

TICKET AGENT: I want to be certain this man belongs to you, Mr. Johnson. Some white people help runaway slaves travel to freedom, so I need you to sign this form.

ELLEN: I can't use my arm. Would you sign the form instead?

TICKET AGENT: I'm sorry sir, I will not sign for you. I don't do favors for strangers.

NARRATOR 2: Ellen didn't know what to do.

READER 1 (as man on boat): Excuse me, sir. I know Mr. Johnson, and this slave does belong to him.

NARRATOR 1: A man from the boat signed the form. Ellen and William were one step closer to freedom. For two more days, William and Ellen traveled by boat and train. Ellen worried about getting to Philadelphia by Christmas Day.

NARRATOR 2: On Christmas Eve, Ellen and William arrived in Baltimore, Maryland. Once again, Ellen got into a car for white passengers. William walked to the car for black people. Then someone tapped him hard on the shoulder.

Next Page — **RAILROAD OFFICER**

RAILROAD OFFICER: Where are you going, boy?

WILLIAM: To Philadelphia, sir. I'm traveling with my master.

RAILROAD OFFICER: Well, you'd better get him into the office. You have to get approval first.

NARRATOR 1: William and Ellen walked to the office. The railroad officer looked serious. He wasn't going to let any slaves escape to the North from his station.

RAILROAD OFFICER: Mr. Johnson, I need proof that this man here belongs to you.

ELLEN: I don't have any proof.

RAILROAD OFFICER: Do you know anyone in Baltimore who can help?

ELLEN: No.

NARRATOR 2: A crowd had gathered outside the office. Ellen tried hard not to panic. What would a white man do? A white man would not be afraid. A white man would be angry. He would demand better treatment. So Ellen did something a slave could never do. She stood up for her rights.

ELLEN: I bought tickets all the way to Philadelphia. You have no right to keep me here!

SOUND: [bell clanging]

RAILROAD OFFICER: I give up. I suppose it's all right.

Next Page — **NARRATOR 1**

NARRATOR 1: William and Ellen hurried onto the train. In a few hours, it would be Christmas Day. Early on Christmas morning, Ellen saw lights in the distance. It was Philadelphia! As soon as the train stopped, William and Ellen climbed off. Ellen looked around at the other passengers. People were laughing and hugging their families.

SOUND: [laughing families]

ELLEN: We can be a family now. We're finally safe. We'll never be slaves again.

ALL: The End

Pronunciation Guide

Baltimore: BALL-tuh-mohr
Macon: MAY-kuhn
Missus: MIS-suhz
Philadelphia: FIL-uh-DEL-fee-uh
Savannah: suh-VAN-uh

Glossary

abolitionism: the movement to end slavery
bundle: a group of things fastened together
cabin: the room in a train for passengers
officer: a person who holds a position of authority
plantation: a large farm where crops are raised
runaway: a slave that has escaped from his or her master
sling: a bandage that hangs from the neck to support an arm
snipped: cut with small, quick strokes
ticket agent: a person who sells tickets

Selected Bibliography

Bolden, Tonya. *And Not Afraid to Dare: The Story of Ten African-American Women*. New York: Scholastic, 1998.

Craft, William. *Running a Thousand Miles for Freedom: The Escape of William and Ellen Craft from Slavery*. 1860. Reprint, Athens: Univ. of Georgia, 1999.

Quarles, Benjamin. *Black Abolitionists*. New York: Oxford Univ. Press, 1969.

Sterling, Dorothy. *Black Foremothers: Three Lives*. New York: Feminist Press, 1988.

Sterling, Dorothy, ed. *We Are Your Sisters: Black Women in the Nineteenth Century*. New York: W. W. Norton, 1984.

Further Reading and Websites

BOOKS

Fradin, Dennis, and Judith Fradin. *5,000 Miles to Freedom: Ellen and William Craft's Flight from Slavery*. Washington, DC: National Geographic Children's Books, 2006.
This book tells the story of the Crafts' escape and their lives afterward. It includes black-and-white photographs, letters, newspapers, and other primary sources.

Knudsen, Shannon. *When Were the First Slaves Set Free during the Civil War?* Minneapolis: Lerner Publications Company, 2010.
This book helps readers learn about the end of slavery in the United States. Find out more about this important moment in U.S. history.

Weidt, Maryann N. *Harriet Tubman*. Minneapolis: Lerner Publications Company, 2003.
Escaped slave Harriet Tubman devoted her life to helping other people find freedom. This book helps readers explore Tubman's life with illustrations, sidebars, a timeline, and more.

WEBSITES

Georgia Stories: William and Ellen Craft
http://www.gpb.org/georgiastories/story/william_and_ellen_craft
Watch a short video feature from Georgia Public Broadcasting about William and Ellen Craft.

National Geographic Online Presents the Underground Railroad
http://www.nationalgeographic.com/railroad/
This site lets visitors learn more about how southern slaves traveled to free states with an interactive game, an escape route map, and more.

National Underground Railroad Network to Freedom
http://home.nps.gov/ugrr/
Read about people across the United States who were involved in slaves struggles for freedom at this site from the National Park Service.

Dear Teachers and Librarians,

Congratulations on bringing Reader's Theater to your students! Reader's Theater is an excellent way for your students to develop their reading fluency. Phrasing and inflection, two important reading skills, are at the heart of Reader's Theater. Students also develop public speaking skills such as volume, pacing, and facial expression.

The traditional format of Reader's Theater is very simple. There really is no right or wrong way to do it. By following these few tips, you and your students will be ready to explore the world of Reader's Theater.

EQUIPMENT

Location: A theater or gymnasium is a fine place for a Reader's Theater performance, but staging the performance in the classroom works well too.

Scripts: Each reader will need a copy of the script. Scripts that are individually printed should be bound into binders that allow the readers to turn the pages easily. Printable scripts for all the books in this series are available at www.historyspeaksbooks.com.

Music Stands: Music stands are very helpful for the readers to set their scripts on.

Costumes: Traditional Reader's Theater does not use costumes. Dressing uniformly, such as all wearing the same color shirt, will give a group a polished look. Specific costume pieces can be used when a reader is performing multiple roles. They help the audience follow the story.

Props: Props are optional. If necessary, readers may mime or gesture to convey objects that are important to the story. Props can be used much like a costume piece to identify different characters performed by one reader. Prop suggestions for each story are available at www.historyspeaksbooks.com.

Background and Sound Effects: These aren't essential, but they can add to the fun of Reader's Theater. Customized backgrounds for each story in this series and sound effects corresponding to the scripts are available at www.historyspeaksbooks.com. You will need a screen or electronic whiteboard for the background. You will need a computer with speakers to play the sound effects.

PERFORMANCE

Staging: Readers usually face the audience in a straight line or a semicircle. If the readers are using music stands, the stands should be raised chest high. A stand should not block a reader's mouth or face, but it should allow for the reader to read without looking down too much. The main character is usually placed in the center. The narrator is on the end. In the case of multiple narrators, place one narrator on each end.

Reading: Reader's Theater scripts do not need to be memorized. However, the readers should be familiar enough with the script to maintain a fair amount of eye contact with the audience. Encourage readers to act with their voices by reading with inflection and emotion.

Blocking (stage movement): For traditional Reader's Theater, there are no blocking cues to follow. You may want to have the students turn the pages simultaneously. Some groups prefer that readers sit or turn their back to the audience when their characters are "offstage" or have left a scene. Some groups will have their readers move about the stage, script in hand, to interact with the other readers. The choice is up to you.

Overture and Curtain Call: Before the performance, a member of the group should announce the title and the author of the piece. At the end of the performance, all readers step in front of their music stands, stand in a line, grasp hands, and bow in unison.

Please visit www.historyspeaksbooks.com for printable scripts, prop suggestions, sound effects, a background image that can be projected on a screen or electronic whiteboard, a Reader's Theater teacher's guide, and reading-level information for all roles.